ELMO'S ALPHABET

By Michaela Muntean
Illustrated by Richard Walz

A SESAME STREET/GOLDEN PRESS BOOK

Published by Western Publishing Company, Inc.,
in conjunction with Children's Television Workshop.

"A, B, C, D, E, F, G," Elmo sang as he and Big Bird walked home from play group.

"That's very good, Elmo," said Big Bird. "Do you know what comes next?"

"Oh, yes! Listen. H, I, J, K, L, M, N, O, P. Elmo knows the *whole* alphabet. Q, R, S, T, U, V...W, X, Y, and Z. Now I know my ABC's, tell me what you think of me."

"I think you're a good friend and an excellent alphabet singer," Big Bird answered.

"Do you want to hear the alphabet song again, Big Bird?" Elmo asked.

"I've got a better idea," said Big Bird. "Let's play our favorite alphabet game."

Aa

airplane

"Okay. Elmo will go first," Elmo said. "Elmo's favorite A word is **airplane**."

Elmo imagined flying an airplane. "Look up, Big Bird. Look up and see Elmo fly an airplane high in the sky."

Bb

boat

"If you look down from your airplane, you will see me in a boat," said Big Bird. "That's because B is for boat. I will be rowing a boat on a beautiful blue lake."

Cc

"C is for **clown**!" cried Elmo. "Elmo would like to be a clown and do funny things to make everyone laugh."

Elmo pictured himself in a clown costume. He wore a pointed hat and big floppy shoes.

clown

drum

Dd

"D is for the drum I will play for you," Big Bird said. "Listen to the drumroll, da-da-da-dum. Here comes Elmo the clown!"

Elmo the clown did a cartwheel while Big Bird played the drum.

Ee

"E is for **engineer**," said Elmo. "Elmo would like to be the engineer driving a train. Woo-woo! Look, everybody, here comes Elmo the engineer."

engineer

"F is for **flag**," said Big Bird. "I am waving a flag. Please stop the train, Mr. Engineer. There are four passengers waiting to get on."

flag

Ff

Gg

"Guess what my favorite G word is?" said Elmo.

"Is it grouch?" Big Bird asked.

"No," said Elmo. "Guess again."

"Grape? Giggle? Goldilocks?" guessed Big Bird.

"No," said Elmo. "It's guitar."

guitar

horn

Hh

"That's great," said Big Bird, "because my favorite H word is horn. Let's get together and play some music, Elmo."

"I is for **ice cream**," said Elmo. "Elmo would like a bowl of ice cream right now."

Ii

ice cream

jar

"And I will bring a jar of marshmallow topping to put on our ice cream," said Big Bird. "J is for **jar**."

Jj

Kk

"Elmo's favorite K word is kite," said Elmo. "Look at Elmo's bright red kite with a long tail. Watch it swoop and soar through the air!"

kite

ladder

Ll

"Oops," said Elmo. "Elmo's kite is caught in a tree."

"Don't worry," said Big Bird. "L is for **ladder**. I always bring along a ladder when we go kite-flying."

Elmo laughed. It was lucky his friend Big Bird was so smart!

Mm

moose

"M is for **moose**," said Elmo. "Elmo would like to meet a moose on Sesame Street. Elmo would say, 'Good morning, Mr. Moose. How are you today?'"

Nn

newspaper

"If you met a moose on Sesame Street," said Big Bird, "that would be big news. I bet you'd get your picture in the newspaper. N is for newspaper."

Oo

ocean

"O is for **ocean**," said Elmo. "Let's go to the ocean, Big Bird."

"Okay," Big Bird agreed. "We'll build sand castles and collect seashells."

The more Elmo thought about the ocean, the more he could feel the warm sun on his fur. He could hear the sound of the waves and smell the salty ocean air.

"Elmo picks **pillow** as Elmo's favorite P word," Elmo said. "Elmo has a soft, fluffy pillow."

"Q is for **quilt**," said Big Bird. "My Granny Bird made me a quilt for my nest."

"Elmo has a good idea," Elmo said. "You could bring your quilt to Elmo's house, and we could have a sleepover!"

Rr

"R is for rocket," said Elmo. "There is room for two in Elmo's rocket. Would you like to come for a ride, Big Bird?"

rocket

Ss

star

"Oh, yes," cried Big Bird. "On the way, we're sure to see some stars. My very favorite S word is star."

Elmo and Big Bird imagined they were racing through space.

Tt

tree

"Elmo's favorite T word is **tree**," Elmo told Big Bird.
"And Elmo's favorite tree is in the park."
Elmo thought about his favorite tree and all the birds
and squirrels who lived there.

"Uh-oh," said Big Bird. "It's starting to rain. I'm glad I remembered to bring my umbrella. U is for **umbrella**."

"We'll stay dry under your umbrella," said Elmo.

Uu

umbrella

Vv

"Elmo knows what V is for," Elmo said. "V is for **valentine**. Elmo likes valentines."

"I like valentines, too," Big Bird said. "I like to get them, and I like to give them."

FEBRUARY

S	M	T	W	T	F	S
		1	2	3	4	5
6	7	8	9	10	11	12
13	14	15	16	17	18	19
20	21	22	23	24	25	26
27	28					

valentine

Ww   Xx   Yy

xylophone

yo-yo

wagon

"Elmo can think of lots of wonderful words that start with the letter W," said Elmo. "Wiggle and window and wish are nice, but wagon is Elmo's favorite. W is for **wagon**."

"What would you put in your wagon?" Big Bird asked.

"Elmo would put a **xylophone** for the letter X, and a **yo-yo** for the letter Y," said Elmo.

"That's very good, Elmo," said Big Bird. "Now there's just one letter left."

Zz

"It's the letter Z," said Elmo. "Z is for **zebra**. Elmo knows where we can see a zebra."

"The zoo!" said Elmo and Big Bird together.

zebra

"Now Elmo is sad because the alphabet game is over,"
Elmo said. "Let's play it again, Big Bird."

"We'll play tomorrow," Big Bird answered. "Right now
I'm ready to go to another favorite H word."

"What's that?" Elmo wanted to know.

"Home," said Big Bird.

"Okeydokey," said Elmo.